Tabitha's Terrifically Tough Tooth

With thanks to my
Mother and Father
and Endaf,
for all their help and support

CM

First published in the United States 2001

by Phyllis Fogelman Books

An imprint of Penguin Putnam Books for Young Readers

345 Hudson Street • New York, New York 10014

Published in 2000 by David & Charles Children's Books, Great Britain

Copyright © 2000 by Charlotte Middleton

All rights reserved. Printed in Singapore

Library of Congress Cataloging-in-Publication Data available upon request

1 3 5 7 9 10 8 6 4 2

Tabitha's Terrifically Tough Tooth

by Charlotte Middleton

Phyllis Fogelman Books · New York

Every morning, Tabitha liked to
finish off her breakfast with an apple.
She took a big bite...

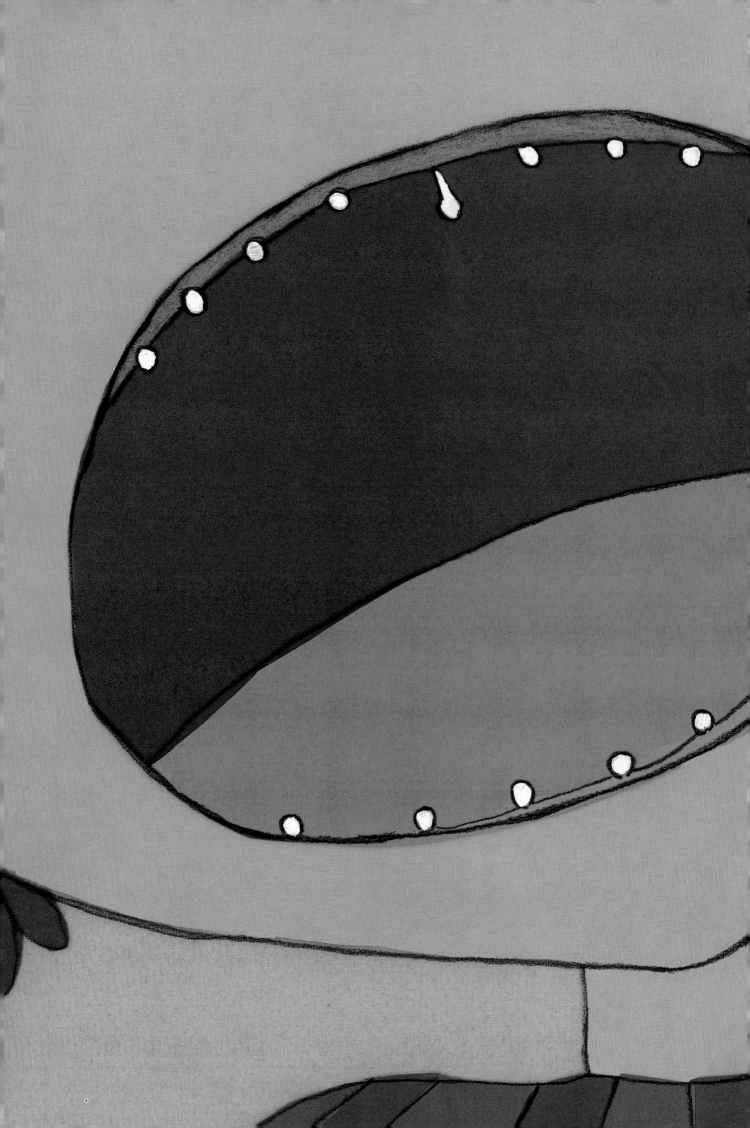

"OW!"

Tabitha had a wobbly tooth!

She smiled at her dad.
Her dad smiled back and said,
"If you put that tooth under your pillow
tonight, the Tooth Fairy will take it
and leave you some money."

Tabitha wanted her
tooth to come out now!
She went upstairs to her
room and put on some music.
Maybe dancing around
would make her tooth fall out...

...but it just made
her hot and tired.

"Huuuum m m m

Tabitha got dressed and went downstairs.
She tied one end of a piece of string
around her tooth and the other end
around her tortoise...

but the tortoise took two steps and fell fast asleep!

Tabitha went to the park and
jumped high on the trampoline.

She hoped that her tooth might bounce out, but it didn't budge!

Back at home she had another idea.
Maybe her dad's Venus flytrap plant could
become a Venus toothtrap...

Now it was getting late and
Tabitha had only one idea left.

She stuck one end of her

extra-chewy bubble gum to her tooth

and the other to the door...

. . .but that didn't work either.

Tabitha was fed up.

She had tried everything she could

think of, and now it was time for bed.

There'd be no visit from the Tooth Fairy tonight.

Then her nose began to tickle,
and her eyes began to itch,
and . . .

aa...

aa...

aaaaaahh...

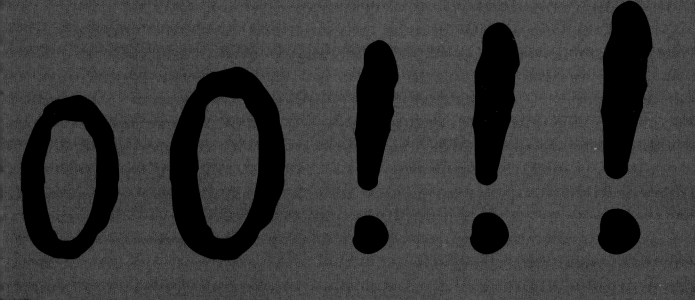

OO!!!!

...out popped Tabitha's tooth!

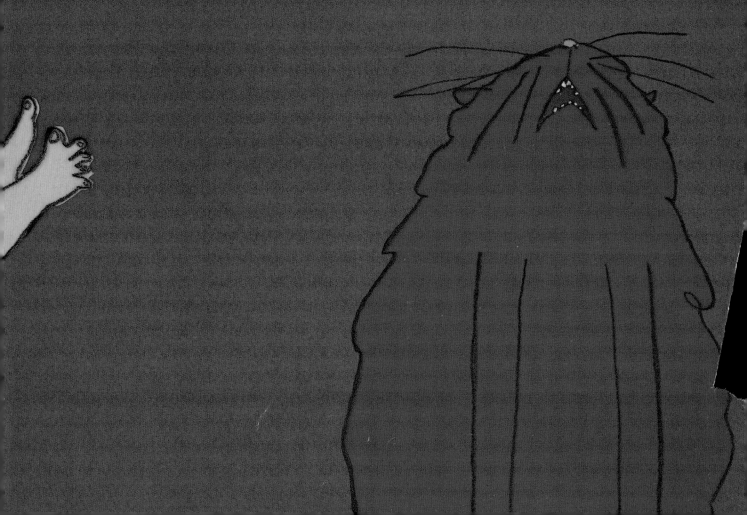